Original title:
The Do Not Fear Stories

Editor: KRISTO VILLEM

ISBN 978-9916-651-01-8

STORIES THROUGH SEASONS

LIZA MOONLIGHT

Greetings, friends! This story will teach you the ever changing flow of time. As time passes, so do the seasons. There are many lovely things to each season and each of them holds many secrets and surprises.

Enjoy these tales and hopefully you will also discover something new!

Everything that surrounds us has patterns. As the day always follows the night and the sun always sets and then rises, the seasons also follow one another. The first season of our book's cycle is Spring. It a time of many new beginnings. Birds return to their homeplaces and the sun start to give more and more warmth. Chippy the Bird will be Your guide!

It is probably no surprise that the thrilly easter rabbit family comes out to enjoy the sun and play around on the warm grass. They have been sitting snugly in their burrows for the whole winter and are so very happy to be outside and hop around and flop their ears.

As the first leaves are turning green, the birds find their favourite spots to to make their nests. Spring is the perfect time to hatch eggs so that bird babies can learn how to fly and explore their own lives.

The cherry trees blossomed and bloomed as white as snow. A cute fat yellow bird flew onto the tree to smell the sweet scent and feel the soft breeze high up on the tallest branch. This made the birdy flap his wings gently.

Candy the young kitten was so relieved that the whole countryside had turned green. She purred and rolled around enthusiastically. She found a tiny lake and bravely went on to have a quick swim in the warm water.

Hoppy the floppy-eared brown rabbit was eagerly waiting for the seeds to start sprouting first leaves out of the earth. She could not wait until the sweet-sweet carrots are finished and she could sink her sharp teeth into them, filling her belly with delicious carrot juice.

As Chippy had been looking at all of these wonderful animals, the Spring had gradually turned to Summer. The weather was now much warmer and everything was in full bloom. Chippy went on to see what kind of adventures the animals of the forest had undertaken. So exciting!

The kitten twins, Mew and Mow had been playing around on an open field when their pal, Roofers the hound dog found them to give them a paw with cleaning up their fur coats. They were newly born kittens and their splendid white coats had gotten dirty from all the rolling and jumping. Roofers was glad to help them out.

The summery days were filled with laughter and games. A tiny mouse spurried across the great open plains, chasing a huge butterfly. This butterfly was multiple times larger than the mouse was, even so the mouse was not afraid to chase after the big bug. It was great fun.

Very near to where the mouse had been playing there were Mr. Zebra and Mrs. Giraffe. They were casually chatting along and discussing the wonderful warm weather. Both of them could graze to their hearts' content. Neither of them had a single worry.

Naturally, no summer is complete without strawberries. Two little colorful butterflied woke up this morning to go out and do a scavenger hunt. The most difficult part was to find the most scrumptious strawberries and that was exactly what they found right next to a lake with the most stunning view. They were both very pleased.

On such a fine day as this, all of the kittens want to run around and play as much as they possibly can. This playful little cat found a colorful ball that was even bigger than himself. This did of course not bother him and he decided to play and have a lot fo fun. The ball was filled with air.

Time passes and along with it, everything and everyone changes too. Chippy's feathers have turned brown as the falling leaves and the impending Fall is just around the corner. Now the days grow shorter and the nights grow colder. Even so, Chippy knows this is not a bad thing, it is just how nature is, was and always will be.

The occasional rain is a welcomed part of Fall. the more rain that pours down the more the late harvest gets to fluorish. Clouds gather and disperse. The strong gusts of wind will eventually shake away the clouds and the rain will have to stop. Sometimes soon, possibly.

Just as the rain had stopped, the two friendly puppies, Spark and Woofa came out of their dog houses to marvel at how the nature had started to show its colors thanks to the abundant water. The usually calm river that flows past their houses was flowing with great speed and they were barking happily as the cool water flowed past them.

If there was one animal who really knew how to enjoy any kind of weather then it was Candy the kitten. She sat in the warm springy yellowish grass, looking at the birds flying past to the South. She liked how the wind was still warm as she yawned calmly, listening to the waterfall right next to where she had been sitting. Such a relaxing sound.

Mr. Zebra and Mrs. Giraffe were still talking, even now. They were discussing how lovely the colorful trees looked. So vibrant. So many colours. Both of them were very keen to find out what kind of a Winter there would be this year. It cannot be long now, they thought. The days were now quite chilly.

Felix the Fox was still a very young fox cub. He did not quite understand why the leaves of all the trees had started to fall off. His mother told him to wait patiently as in time all the questions will be answered.

Chippy was wise to know that the more he flew about, the more warm he would be. Birds do not have to worry about the cold so long as they keep moving. The Winter had come. A nice friendly kid had made a snowman right next to Chippy's favourite fence and he added a carrot for the funky looking snowman so that it would be complete.

One thing that all of the animals of this forest always looked forward to was that in the winter time, the night sky would oftern light up in very beautiful colours. All the animals would gather around to see this spectacle. It was something they would only see in Winter.

You have probably heard of the mighty Mammoths. This mammoth was angry at how the tiny people always stepped on his tail. He thought they would all see the furry creature's tail but was so fluffy that it wiggled and wagged around in the wintery breeze. This human wearing a red hat bumped into the mammoth and there was nothing he could do . He was simply that big.

Even though Emma the wolf mother knew well that howling might frrighten other citizens of the forest, she could not help herself when she saw the full moon of the December sky. It excited her to be able to send out word to all of the other animals to look up into the sky. Not many look at the sky at all, don't you agree?

When morning arrived, Emma was still howling. She had gotten too excited and had trouble pulling the breaks. Luckily the old wise moose Manfred was just walking past Emma and suggested that she dug her nose in the cold snow. She tried it and the cold snow helped her calm down.

Our story of the Seasons has come to an end but before we call it a close, leave it to Chippy to bring you the moral of this story. Bear this is in mind:

Everything in your life is in ever lasting change. Nothing you know will always stay the same. It is important to accent that letting go is something we must learn and the more we let go of the old, the more room will be born. Even if the future is sometimes scary. Stay healthy!

Fey the Magical Fairy

Liza Moonlight

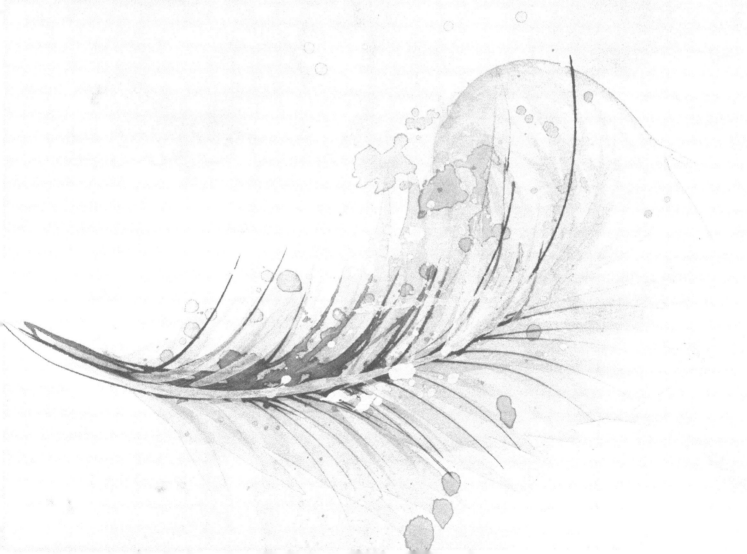

Meet Fey. She is known to be one of the most cheerful fairies in the entire world. Fairies are the ones who uphold the light on Earth. However, Fey grew bored of her innate talent and the mission she was given at birth.

You see, all young fairies have a common dream. They dream to become a part of human society and see what life is like when you live among people. This course in a fairie's life always comes with a risk, however. They might lose their creativity.

To fulfill her life long dream, Fey would need to find a human girl who had a similar dream to hers - the child would dream of becoming a fairy. They would then switch places in the two worlds, the human world and The Fairyland, where Fey lived.

he sent out her trusty steed, Bella the Unicorn to fetch her
nformation about young human girls who dreamed of
ecoming fairies. Surely, this must be an easy task, Fey thought,
s she bid Bella farewell.

Just as Fey had predicted, it only took Bella a short stroll in the
human world, when she found a little girl in a valley, standing
bare footed with paper mache wings and wishing she could fly
just as in her dreams.

Bella sent out a signal to Fey and in the blink of an eye, the part of us which we commonly call the creativity, flew straight from Fey to the little girl. Fey cast a spell towards the girl and in the blink of an eye, they had switched places in the two worlds.

Fey was just preparing to be transported to the human world when a fairy elephant charged on over. He was then transported along with Fey and they soon woke up in the sunny forest far beyond their home the Fairyland.

Hooters the Elephant soon became accustomed to the lush forests of Earth. Both him and Fey took the most of life as the main difference between life on Earth and back home was that everyone had to find their own purpose in life all by themselves.

It was not long before Fey grew bored of the life on Earth. Everything was so plain and simple to her. She summoned a bird to carry her message to Fey's sister. Fey wished to ask her sister to bring her back home so that she could once again send light to planet Earth, albeit from afar.

Fey's sister, Ariana, received work from Fey as the earthly bird had morphed into a fairy bird to cross the realms. Ariana was very happy to hear that her sister would return soon. She sent out the word so that everyone would know.

However, Fey's evil step mother would also hear of this news. She had always been jealous of Fey's natural beauty and her shine. She wanted to stop Fey from returning and to do that, she would have hide the gateway back to Fairyland.

For the gateway to Fairyland to be hidden, Fey's evil step mother asked her henchman, Erna the Evil Fairy, to dim down the light in the Magical Lantern. It was the source of light that shone brightly to all who travel between the two worlds.

Erna did as she was told and also hid the lantern away. It had been kept in the Lantern Cottage for thousands of years. Now however, the mischevous fairy took it to the Great Tower so that noone could possibly reach it.

Fey had many friends. Her sister asked the famous hero Elrond to aid our friend-in-need. The might hero forged a plan to rescue the Lantern from the Great Tower. Elron managed to retreive the Lantern, but something was off, he could just feel it.

Even as the lantern has been brought back from the ominous tower, Fey the lovable fairy was nowhere to be seen. Life passed as ever and some had thought that Fey had deliberately decided to stay behind on Earth.

Seasons changed and winter followed autumn. Spring followed soon after and the summer had bloomed twice. All in good time, though, Fey fluttered down the snowy mountains of Fairyland to revisit her friends and family. This was a big surprise.

Truth be told, Fey knew fair well that she could return to he
homeland. The reason for staying behind was that she knew o
the little girl who had become a fairy in her stead. She enjoyec
the life in Fairyland so much that Fey did not have the heart to
bring her back to Earth.

As the years had passed, Fey had also learned to enjoy life on Earth. She shared her kindness with everyone and learned to love those around her. When the young human girl returned home to her family, she no longer dreamed of becoming a fairy but to raise her own family and teach her children about everything she had learned during her time in Fairyland.

When Fey had reached her own home, just beneath the che[rry] trees, she felt a rush of creativity. She had not felt it the la[st] time when she lived in Fairyland. This helped her realize tha[t] change in scenery can truly boost our liveliness and teach [us] how to enjoy life as we do when we are young children. Enjoyi[ng] life to the fullest is a very important aspect to achieving o[ur] goals. Fey knew this well.

Fey knew that to live out her full potential in life would mean to stay connected with herself and know what her true calling in life is. It is to spread light and love as a fairy and to stay close with those who loved her unconditionally.

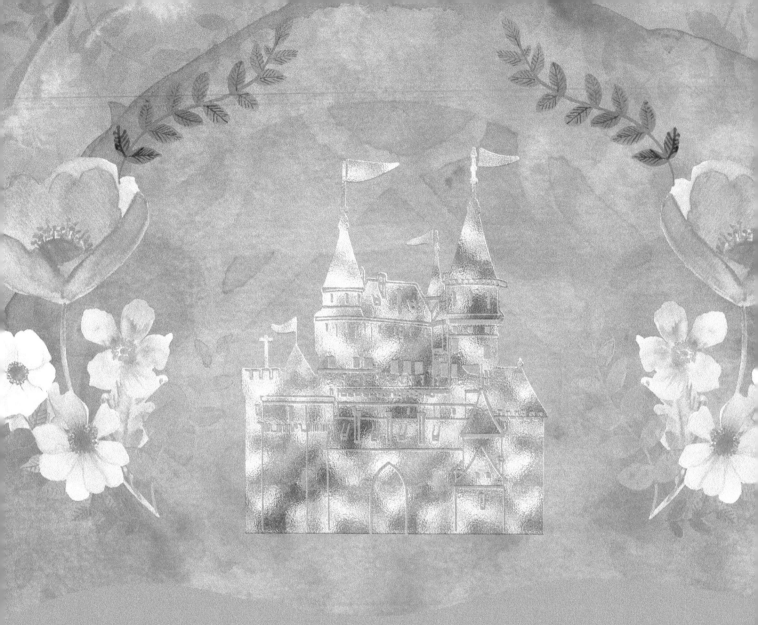

As you might think, Elrond the mighty hero also liked Fey a lot and as soon as she returned to Fairyland, Elrond asked for her hand in marriage. Fey, naturally, accepted and so the two wonderful fairies got married to live out their lives in the great Castle of Imagination. They lived happily ever after.

Milo The Sheep

Learn To Trust Life

Liza Moonlight

Milo the Sheep was the fluffiest, most cheerful lamb You could possibly imagine. One could even say he was too brave.

He was the most trusting animal in the whole forest and many questioned if he was perhaps too trusting. This unfolding adventure put his trust to the test.

Milo lived by a lake with his mother. One day, however, as Milo woke up, his mother was nowhere to be found. He decided this was the right time to go off and find where mama had gone. The day was sunny and the birds were chirping softly.

The nearby meadows were bewildering. All the beauty of the nature had blossomed and Milo felt like a newly born little lamb, frollocking around in the soft squishy mud and feeling the warm sunlight on his wool coat. He knew it's not good to wander off but this nature was so very inviting. He ventured further from home.

On the verge of his homely forest, he found an old wooden cabin. A great yellow cat sat by the cabin and Milo asked if the kitty had seen his mother. The cheeky cat looked at this jolly lamb and told him to head south. Milo followed his advice without suspecting anything fishy.

Milo reached the very edge of the forest all to find an old boat.
Oh what joy, the lamb thought and hopped on the boat and start
moving upstream toward where the cat had pointed.

Rowing on the old crooked boat took Milo the rest of the day and he thought taking a rest would be the best idea. Although Milo still hadn't found a single clue about where his mother might be, he did not hesitate to travel on as he knew that the trust he had in life would eventually carry him to his goals.

He gazed at the sunset and the beauty of this unbelieveably wonderful natural light show. He felt truly grateful of all the places he had visited this day. The friendly cat that had guided him to such a gorgeous spot and the dreams that he would see soon enough.

A new day had dawned and Milo found himself an intriguing path ahead. A tall strong rocky brick bridge towered above the nature and trees. This would be the best place to look far and wide to unceoover the whereabouts of his mother, Milo thought.

The end of the bridge lead Milo to an abandoned stone house. Inside the house, he found pieces of wool. So although he did not see mama from high up, the pieces of wool in this house must mean that mama was nearby, right?

Finding the pieces of wool gave Milo even more courage and enthusiasm to go and see more places before eventually finding his mama. He reached a breathtaking sight - a great big mountain lay infront of him just next to a pond of cooling fresh mountain water.

Well what do you know! Milo was not the only one ready to take a sip from the frest source of water. A pack of wild horses neared Milo from the distance. It was a hot day so at first, he thought his eyer were deceiving him. Yet, it was true and the horses were friendly.

The horses had heard of a friendly bunny rabbit living in these parts. This rabbit was known for having sharp eyes and seeing all that happens in the forest. Milo took a nice drink from the lake and became wery thrilled to find this exciting rabbit.

Milo did not have to look too far, just behind the tall trees was a flickering sight of a carrot. Milo had once again no doubt that this carrot would belong to the wise little rabbit. Unfortunately, the bunny had not seen a sheep in these parts but told Milo to keep looking.

Milo was slightly daunted by the fact that even the wise rabbit could not help him. Slow and steady, he thought and decided to take the search from the top. He went to visit the farm where both he and his mama had grown up. Then, he heard a loud moo and followed it.

The closer Milo got to the familiar sound, the more he remembered journeys from his childhood as him and his mama came to this grassland to visit their family friend Elsid. Elsid and her daughter Miru were just beyond a spectacularly crafted old bridge.

Elsid and Miru were grazing in their usual spot, just above a cliff on a beautiful flower-filled grassland. Elsid was very glad to see Milo and when she heard of the lamb's trouble, she laughed lightly and asked if he had bothered to wait a few minutes before deciding that his mother had gone missing. Perhaps he was behind a tree somewhere.

Now that Milo thought of it, he had never once thought that th
journey would not lead him to his mama. Not a single doubt in hi
mind, though, how and when he would arrive to his goal, was nc
important. He started his jolly trip back towards home.

o further he got, the more certain and trustful he got that he will
neet mama as soon as he got home. There was, of course, never a
ertainty that he would find what he was looking for. Trust in life was
ll that he could muster.

The flowers bloomed brightly as he skipped along the path
grabbing a bite to eat now and then. he was now close to home and
so very excited to tell his mama all about his long journey. He knew
his mama was not worried, but rather happy to see Milo.

Oh what a happy moment! Milo found his mother right on the other side of the home pond. His mama sat quietly just to listen to her little lamb's stories and marvel at where he had been, She was genuinely happy for her child's adventures. She knew Milo would find his way back home and that's what's important,

As the two sheep reunited, the jolly wise rabbit looked from afar an
feld glad for them. Milo had learned how to have no expectation
for life. **What we imagine is what we will eventually get, tha
is the biggest truth in life and the rabbit was happy to hav
shared this secret with his new friend.**

Shaggy The Lost Furry

Liza Moonlight

Meet Shaggy, the kindhearted little Furry. He is the clumsiest creature in all of Furryland.

He has the heart the size of an the Sun. His body is soft and shaped like squishy sausage.

His face is brown and his dark eyes make you feel very warm inside. His gently wagging tail reflects his pure soul and his ears are soft and fluffy.

haggy lives in the wonderfully colorful Aquarelle world. It is a place where the joy and colors play gleefully in the warm wind and the laughter of every single moment echoes on ever so brightly.

However, Shaggy sometimes felt a little bit down in the dumps. You see, he did not have any other Furries to play with. All of his friends and neighbours were quite different than he was. He wished he had friends like himself.

Shaggy had always dreamt of floating freely in the ocean without worrying about his fur getting wet. Even a boat would not guarantee that his fur would not get soaked!

Snappy the playful crocodile came togreet Shaggy and told him he does not have to worry about getting wet. If he needs something from the great wide ocean ther Snappy would be more than happy to bring it to him.

Shaggy wished he had a big enough mouth to store enough water so that he could sprinkle it all on the pretty flowers of the forest.

Heyho the Hippopotamus had a large mouth and calmed Shaggy down by promising to sprinkle the water of a nearby waterfall onto all the flowers of the forest.

Shaggy became a little bit weary and went for a stroll in the forest. The sun was shining so very brightly and he wished he could lay in the warm sunlight all day and not be so busy

Snape the Snake whizzed over to our friendly Furry and told him to fret not. There are animals who could only dream of being as busy as Shaggy was. He should be proud to be able to meet so many different animals all the time

The next day, Shaggy stumbled upon a group of tiny islands in the middle of a large lake. He saw someone afar, stomping the ground. He imagined how nice it would be to have his very own island. Nice and private.

Phanto the Elephant was the one Shaggy was smiling at. Phanto told Shaggy that having your own island was not all fun and games. It can be lonely and sometimes you need to go to the main land for groceries.

Right on the next island, Shaggy saw a peculiar looking animal. It was Gina the Giraffe. She seemed happy as ever! Looking all tall and mighty, she saw far and wide.

Gina saw Shaggy from a distance and waved politely with her tiny colorful ears. Shaggy and Gina made a deal that whenever Shaggy would feel like seeing further from high up, then the giraffe wouldtake him on her back for a ride.

A nice old cabin stood strong and proud on the edge of the local forest. Shaggy wondered who lived there. As he got closer, he heard the folks of the cabin discussing about their lost pony, Zara.

Shaggy quickly found the feisty pony in the nearby woods. Zara was practicing her long jumps. She did not have enough room to do so at the farm. Shaggy thought that everyone's life might not be as pretty as on first glance.

he fluffy Furry Shaggy reached the edge of a great rilliantly clear lake. The water was so clear that one could asily get thirsty just from the sight of it.

Right that moment, Sam the Lion rushed out of the woods. The hot day had made him thirsty, much unlike the king of the wild. Shaggy saw that even Sam has basic needs.

t has been a very long day. Luckily, Shaggy found a nice cozy bench to sit on and think about what he had seen and learned. It is crutial to take time every day to think about what new you have experienced and learned.

Shaggy slowly became sleepy while looking at the setting sun, the slow village life drift past into night mode. He knew that he would learn a lot in the dream world as soon as he went to sleep.

The moment Shaggy closed his eyes, hundreds and hundreds of hot air balloons, all shapes and sizes, started appearing. They were so mezmerising that for a second, he forgot to make conclusions based on his day.

However, Shaggy knew that the dreamtime is best fo
making realizations. He learned from magical sight th
everyone is special in their own right. We are all unique ar
it is important to love ourselves for it. Do not forget that.

CAM
Creative Arts Management

Thank You for reading This Book!

To show our **appreciation**,
here is a
FREE additional **Story**!

Download at:

www.creativeartsmanagement.org/
getabook/

CPSIA information can be obtained
at www.ICGtesting.com
Printed in the USA
BVHW021751270421
605960BV00005B/242

9 789916 651018